The Shepherd Girl
of Bethlehem

For Kim and Laurel,
and all the brave daughters   C.M.

Text copyright © 2011 Carey Morning
Illustrations copyright © 2011 Alan Marks
This edition copyright © 2011 Lion Hudson

The moral rights of the author and illustrator
have been asserted

A Lion Children's Book
an imprint of
Lion Hudson plc
Wilkinson House, Jordan Hill Road,
Oxford OX2 8DR, England
www.lionhudson.com
ISBN 978 0 7459 6232 0

First edition 2011
1 3 5 7 9 10 8 6 4 2 0

A catalogue record for this book is available
from the British Library

Typeset in 20/24 Elegant Garamond BT
Printed in China July 2011 (manufacturer LH06)

Distributed by:
UK: Marston Book Services Ltd, PO Box 269, Abingdon, Oxon OX14 4YN
USA: Trafalgar Square Publishing, 814 N Franklin Street, Chicago, IL 60610
USA Christian Market: Kregel Publications, PO Box 2607, Grand Rapids, MI 49501

The Shepherd Girl
of Bethlehem

Carey Morning

Illustrated by Alan Marks

LION
CHILDREN'S

Her father was a shepherd.
She was almost always with him,
tending their sheep.

He needed her.

When he found a lost lamb,
he would tuck it in her lap.
She would let it suck her fingers
until its mother came back.

When he sheared the sheep,
she would gather up the fleece
and stuff the big sacks until they were full...

and bouncy!

And sometimes, while her father dozed on the hill,
she would tend the flock all by herself
until he woke and called,

"Where's my little shepherd girl?"

So every dawn he took her along,
and every afternoon.
But every evening, when she asked, "May I come?"
he always answered, "No, it's too dark."
And he kissed her and sent her to bed.

From her window she watched him striding away,
up the hill and on into her dreams.

But on this night, she couldn't sleep.
It wasn't dark! Not dark at all!

The light of a big star filled her room

and lit the whole wide world outside.

So up she got and out she went
into the big bright night alone.

She knew the way:

past the bare bones of the fig tree — clackety-clack!
under the almond tree — billowing blooms!

on through the deep grass – whispering whish!
up through the olive groves – up and up!

At last she reached the flock.
"Papa! Papa!" she called.
But only sheep answered.
"Maaaa! Maaaa!"

She ran up the slope.
"Papa! PAPA!" she yelled.
But only the wind answered.
"Shhhh! Shhhh!"

She climbed to the top.
"PAPA! PAPA!" she howled.
But only her panting breath replied.
"Huh! Huh! Huh! Huh!"

Then she saw him!
Far, far below on the track in the starlight,
he was hurrying off
with a small band of shepherds.

She looked back at the flock,
and down at the village
where her mother was sleeping.
She took a deep breath,
then she turned and ran fast
down the path toward her father.

She leaped over shadows.
She ducked under boughs.
She hiked up her skirt

and the dust flew behind her.

She followed them on and on and on
through the bright night.

Across the hills, behind the inn,
and out to the stable
beneath the glimmering star.

She slipped inside, unseen, behind them.
A cow and a donkey stood side by side.
She squeezed in between their warm shaggy bodies.
It was a cosy, safe place to hide.

Camel bells suddenly jingled outside.
The little door opened.
Purple and velvet and gold swished past.

Then all was silent.
She smelled incense.
She smelled roses.

A white wing unfolded.
And everything shone in a soft golden light.

But where was her father?
She peeked out and whispered, "Papa?"

Kings and shepherds then turned around.
They bent down, smiling.
They took her small hand.
They ushered her forward gently.

And there was her father.
He opened his arms.
"It's not dark tonight, Papa! Not dark at all!"
"You're right," he whispered. "Come. Here is the Light."
And he lifted her up to see.

In his mother's arms a baby lay shining,
the most radiant baby that could ever be.
The baby and the child gazed at each other,
while everyone watched them quietly.

Father and daughter, hand in hand,
crossed the hills homeward in the first light of dawn.
"The baby is brighter than the sun," she said.
"And Papa, his light is inside me now."
"You're right," he said, "and it's yours to keep."

She was happy and tired and wanted to sleep.
So he picked her up, and she closed her eyes
and was filled with the light of her own sunrise.

Other titles from Lion Children's Books

The Animals' Christmas   *Elena Pasquali & Giuliano Ferri*
The Fourth Wise Man   *Mary Joslin & Richard Johnson*
Leah's Christmas Story   *Margaret Bateson-Hill & Karin Littlewood*